Hello, Family Members,

Learning to read is one of the most important accomplishments of early childhood. **Hello Reader!** books are designed to help children become skilled readers who like to read. Beginning readers learn to read by remembering frequently used words like "the," "is," and "and"; by using phonics skills to decode new words; and by interpreting picture and text clues. These books provide both the stories children enjoy and the structure they need to read fluently and independently. Here are suggestions for helping your child *before, during,* and *after* reading:

Before

- Look at the cover and pictures and have your child predict what the story is about.
- Read the story to your child.
- Encourage your child to chime in with familiar words and phrases.
- Echo read with your child by reading a line first and having your child read it after you do.

During

- Have your child think about a word he or she does not recognize right away. Provide hints such as "Let's see if we know the sounds" and "Have we read other words like this one?"
- Encourage your child to use phonics skills to sound out new words.
- Provide the word for your child when more assistance is needed so that he or she does not struggle and the experience of reading with you is a positive one.
- Encourage your child to have fun by reading with a lot of expression . . . like an actor!

After

- Have your child keep lists of interesting and favorite words.
- Encourage your child to read the books over and over again. Have him or her read to brothers, sisters, grandparents, and even teddy bears. Repeated readings develop confidence in young readers.
- Talk about the stories. Ask and answer questions. Share ideas about the funniest and most interesting characters and events in the stories.

I do hope that you and your child enjoy this book.

—Francie Alexander
Chief Education Officer,
Scholastic Education

Go to scholastic.com for web site information
on Scholastic authors and illustrators.

ISBN 0-439-44334-2

Library of Congress Cataloging-in-Publication Data available

Copyright © 2002 by Hans Wilhelm, Inc.

10 9 8 7 6 5 4 3 2 1   02 03 04 05 06

Printed in the U.S.A.   24
First printing, October 2002

I'M NOT SCARED!

by Hans Wilhelm

Hello Reader! — Level 1

SCHOLASTIC INC. Cartwheel B·O·O·K·S ®

New York   Toronto   London   Auckland   Sydney
Mexico City   New Delhi   Hong Kong   Buenos Aires

It's Halloween!
It's time to dress up.

What should I be?

Maybe I should be a funny clown with big feet.

Should I be a bad, bad pirate . . .

or a barking robot?

Maybe I'll be a big, black bat.

Should I be a scary wolf . . .

or a cute little bunny?

Do you like me as
a silly, slimy sea serpent?

Should I be a wise wizard . . .

or an orange pumpkin?

Maybe I should be a mummy.

I know! I will be Super Dog,
and I'll save the world.

Uh-oh! What is this?

Oh, no!

I am scared
of ghosts.

But these are not
real ghosts!

These are my friends!
They are here to play!

Next year I'll give
THEM a scare!